For Lidia Re

THIS IS A BORZOI BOOK PUBLISHED BY ALFRED A. KNOPF.
Copyright © 2015 by Jarrett J. Krosoczka. All rights reserved. Published in the United States by Alfred A. Knopf,
an imprint of Random House Children's Books, a division of Penguin Random House LLC, New York.
Knopf, Borzoi Books, and the colophon are registered trademarks of Penguin Random House LLC. Visit us on the Web! randomhousekids.com.
Educators and librarians, for a variety of teaching tools, visit us at RHTeachersLibrarians.com.

Library of Congress Cataloging-in-Publication Data
Krosoczka, Jarrett J., author, illustrator.   It's tough to lose your balloon / Jarrett J. Krosoczka. — First edition.
p. cm.   Summary: Illustrations and simple text suggest ways to see the positive side of difficulties, from losing one's
balloon to being left with a new babysitter.   ISBN 978-0-385-75479-8 (trade) — ISBN 978-0-385-75480-4 (lib. bdg.) —
ISBN 978-0-385-75481-1 (ebook)   [1. Optimism—Fiction.] I. Title. II. Title: It is tough to lose your balloon.
PZ7.K935It 2015   [E]—dc23   2014032546

The text of this book is set in 30-point Clarendon Roman.   MANUFACTURED IN MALAYSIA   September 2015
10 9 8 7 6 5 4 3 2 1
First Edition

it's tough to lose your balloon

Jarrett J. Krosoczka

Alfred A. Knopf
new york

It's tough to
lose your balloon . . .

. . . but it'll make
Grandma smile
from the sky.

It's sad to
drop your sandwich
in the sand . . .

. . . but it'll make
some seagulls
very happy.

It's never fun when
you break a toy . . .

. . . but you'll have fun fixing it with Grandpa.

It's the worst to
have wet shoes . . .

. . . but it's the best
to go barefoot.

It's frustrating when
your ice cream melts . . .

. . . but your cone
will make a great hat
for your scoop.

It hurts to get
a scrape . . .

. . . but you'll get a cool bandage.
(It might even glow
in the dark!)

It's scary when
you have a new
babysitter . . .

. . . but you get to
stay up late.

So when life gives you rain . . .

...look for the rainbow!

Author's Note

In 1999, when I was a senior at
Rhode Island School of Design, I wrote a book
called "Peanut Butter and Jelly Sandwiches in the
Sand," which listed the injustices of childhood. But there
was no happy ending for each calamity. Many years later,
I found my own happy ending with my wife and our children.
One day we were at a local park when my daughter lost her
balloon. She was devastated. My wife, Gina, comforted Zoe by
telling her that Grandma and Grandpa were flying home
from vacation and they'd see the balloon from
their airplane. It calmed our daughter's
nerves and re-sparked an old
story that had lain dormant
in my studio drawer.